A NOTE TO PARENTS

One of the most important ways childre............................ like reading — is by being with readers. Every t................................. j, or listen to your child read, you are providing t............. that sne or he needs as an emerging reader.

Disney's First Readers were created to make that reading time fun for you and your child. Each book in this series features characters that most children already recognize from popular Disney films. The familiarity and appeal of these high-interest characters will draw emerging readers easily into the story and at the same time support basic literacy skills, such as understanding that print has meaning, connecting oral language to written language, and developing cueing systems. And because Disney's First Readers are highly visual, children have another tool to help in understanding the text. This makes early reading a comfortable, confident experience — exactly what emerging readers need to become successful, fluent readers.

Read to Your Child

Here are a few hints to make early reading enjoyable and educational:

★ Talk with children before reading. Let them see how much they already know about the Disney characters. If they are unfamiliar with the movie basis of a book, take a few minutes to look at the cover and some of the illustrations to establish a context. Talking is important, since oral language precedes and supports reading.

★ Run your finger along the text to show that the words carry the story. Let your child read along if she or he recognizes that there are repeated words or phrases.

★ Encourage questions. A child's questions are good clues to his or her comprehension or thinking strategies.

★ Be prepared to read the same book several times. Children will develop ease with the story and concepts, so that later they can concentrate on reading and language.

Let Your Child Read to You

You are your child's best audience, so encourage her or him to read aloud to you often. And:

★ If children ask about an unknown word, give it to them. Don't interrupt the flow of reading to have them sound it out. However, if children start to sound out a word, let them.

★ Praise all reading efforts warmly and often!

—Patricia Koppman
Past President
International Reading Association

For Lauren,
and for all of us
connected in the great Circle of Life.
— G.T.

Paints and pencils by Sol Studios

Printed in the United States of America

First Edition

1 3 5 7 9 10 8 6 4 2

Library of Congress Catalog Card Number: 98-84128

ISBN: 0-7868-4228-8

SIMBA'S POUNCING LESSON

by Gail Tuchman
Illustrated by Sol Studios

Disney's First Readers — Level 2
A Story from Disney's *The Lion King*

DiSNEY PRESS

New York

In the jungle
of monkeys and trees,
and swinging vines,
and a cooling breeze,
came a cry from Timon.

"Eeeeee-yaaaa!
Charge . . . Pumbaa!"

But when they saw Simba,
the two stopped short.
"What are you doing, kid?"
Pumbaa asked with a snort.

"Pouncing," answered Simba,
"but I missed."

"Aw, Timon," said Pumbaa.
"Let's help our cub.
He needs a little lesson
in getting some grub."

"All righty!
Here's how to pounce,"
Timon pointed out,
as he tiptoed about
on Pumbaa's snout.

"First, tiptoe, nice and slow.
Then, pounce—ready, set, go!"

"OK," said Simba.
"I'll give it a shake.
Watch me pounce
on that big snake."

Simba said to himself,
First, tiptoe, nice and slow.
Then, pounce—ready, set, go!

In the jungle
of monkeys and trees,
and swinging vines,
and a cooling breeze,
the snake hissed.

Simba missed.

"This time," said Pumbaa,
"pretend you're a spy
and follow that fly.
Creep close, then leap high."

"OK," said Simba.
"I'll give it a try.
I'll pounce on that fly,
as easy as pie!"

Simba said to himself,
I'll pretend I'm a spy
and follow that fly.
Creep close, then leap high.

In the jungle
of monkeys and trees,
and swinging vines,
and a cooling breeze,
Simba sneezed.

The fly flew away,
very pleased.

"Try again, kid,"
Timon called out,
as he bounced about
on Pumbaa's snout.

"It's the bounce
that counts
when you pounce!"

"OK," said Simba.
"Let me see.
I'll pounce on that bug,
one, two, three!"

Simba said to himself,
*It's the bounce
that counts
when I pounce!*

In the jungle
of monkeys and trees,
and swinging vines,
and a cooling breeze,
the bug dug.

It had crawled free when
it heard Simba counting,
"One, two, three!"

Tiptoe. Bounce. Spy.
Creep. Leap. Oh, my!
Words spun around in Simba's head.
Then he remembered what his father had said:

"Stay low to the ground,
    and don't make a sound."
        So Simba *quietly*
            practiced pouncing around.

Pumbaa and Timon
were sniffing for ants.
Simba hid and watched
from behind some plants.
Here was his chance!

The cub stayed low to the ground,
and without making a sound . . .

. . . Simba shot out
from the bushes and pounced.
"GOTCHA!"
the cub proudly announced.

"Good surprise, kid,"
said Pumbaa with a groan.
"Great pouncing," moaned Timon.

In the jungle
of monkeys and trees,
and swinging vines,
and a cooling breeze,
came a cry.
"Eeeeee-yaaaa!
HOORAY . . . Simba!"